No Cupcakes for Jason

A Child's Story about the Gluten-free Casein-free Diet

With a Parents' Guide and a School Guide included

Written by Judith Crane and Stephanie Harlan
Illustrated by Kevin Harlan

Introduction written by Betsy Hicks and John Hicks, MD

First published by AuthorHouse 04/20/05

ISBN: 1-4208-4552-7 (sc)

Library of Congress Control Number: 2005903025

Printed in the United States of America
Bloomington, Indiana

This book is printed on acid-free paper.

authorHOUSE

1663 LIBERTY DRIVE
BLOOMINGTON, INDIANA 47403
(800) 839-8640
www.authorhouse.com

Introduction

There are many social challenges for a child who is on a gluten and casein-free diet. Often when they begin, the child feels as if the diet is a punishment. This book serves as a wonderful tool in explaining that diet can add to diversity the same way a different skin color, or language can. Additionally, the book brings awareness to remind us that although our bodies are unique, our desires to "fit in" and enjoy the socialization that food brings is inherent.

Through proper education we can learn that our *differences* are minor compared to the magnitude of our *similarities*. A dairy-free ice cream needs to be no more unusual than a different flavor. Acceptance and encouragement of each child is our duty and obligation as adults. This book provides resources so that anyone can become aware and proficient in these special needs. It should be mandatory reading in every classroom that has a child on any type of special diet.

Betsy and John Hicks, M.D., F.A.A.P.

Author's Note

The information contained in this book should not be taken as medical advice. It is our recommendation that any special diet be started under the advisement of a medical doctor. Each child has unique biological circumstances and should be treated accordingly. This book does not imply a cure from any neurological, physiological, or other disorders that may be described in this book.

Dedicated to Justin -
A real-life kindergartner who
inspires us all...

My name is Jason.
I am five years, six months, and eighteen days old.
I live with my Mommy, my Daddy, two cats,
and one goldfish.

I love to swing.
I love to ride my bike.
I love having my friends come over
to play in my backyard.

A few days ago the ice cream truck
came down my street.
All of the kids ran home to get money.
Not me, though.
I can't eat ice cream.

I started kindergarten this year. I love it!
Tomorrow is Joshua's birthday.
He's bringing cupcakes to school.
None for me, though.
I can't eat cupcakes.

Sometimes, when all the other kids are eating ice cream and cupcakes and other special treats, I want to cry.

I want to be just like all the other kids.

I want to eat ice cream and cupcakes and cookies and pizza and all the other special treats…
…*but I can't.*

I can't eat anything with GLUTEN or CASEIN in it.

Gluten is in cupcakes, cookies, pizza, bread, bagels,
and lots of other foods.

Casein is in ice cream, milk, cheese, yogurt,
and lots of other foods.

If I eat anything with gluten or casein in it,
I feel sick or kind of weird! My Mommy says I act "spacey".
Sometimes I feel angry or I can't fall asleep.

I don't like the way I feel and act when I eat
foods with gluten or casein in them.

But you know what?

There are lots of special stores that sell foods
that *are* safe for me to eat!

And my Grandma bakes really yummy bread and cookies and
muffins and pizza and a lot of other food
that *is* safe for me to eat!

I have special toothpaste and glue and paint,
because sometimes gluten is in things other than food.
I even help Mommy make special gluten-free
play-dough that my whole kindergarten class can use!

So now, when kids bring birthday cupcakes to school,
I can bring my own gluten-free cupcakes from home!
And when I get invited to pizza parties,
I can bring my own special pizza to eat!

And if someone offers me something to eat
that I am not sure is safe, I can say,
"No, thanks!"
because I'd rather not get sick.

I like feeling healthy. I like being happy!
It's not so hard being on a special diet!

I can be just like all the other kids in kindergarten.

I am so happy being me!!

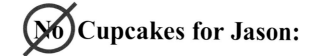

No Cupcakes for Jason:

A Parents' Guide to the GFCF Diet

"My name is Jason. I am five years, six months, and eighteen days old."

And so begins the story of Jason, a little boy who has just begun kindergarten. As he tells his story, he shares all the things that make him happy, such as playing with his friends, riding his bike, and going to school.

But sometimes Jason is not very happy. In fact, sometimes he feels so sad that he wants to cry. He wants to be like all the other kids. But when the other kids eat ice cream, or birthday cupcakes, or go to pizza parties, he feels left out. He cannot eat regular ice cream or regular cake or regular pizza. He cannot eat any food that has gluten or casein in it.

Gluten is a protein that is found in many grains, such as wheat, barley, rye, malt, and oats. Casein is a protein in cows' milk, and can therefore be found in milk, cheese, ice cream, yogurt, and butter. Jason has what is commonly called a "leaky gut".

The leaky gut syndrome is thought to have many causes - excessive use of antibiotics, certain medications, environmental toxins, overgrowth of yeast or bacteria in the intestinal lining, the continual eating of allergenic foods, and many others. Over time, the intestinal lining may become more permeable, allowing these proteins to escape into the bloodstream. If these proteins are not digested completely, they may be partially broken down into peptide chains. These chains then connect to opiate receptors in the brain, thus causing the "spacey" or drugged appearance shared by so many children who ought to be on the diet. Other reactions may include hyperactivity, aggression, poor eye contact, aloofness, social withdrawal, and other behavioral problems.

Some disorders which may respond favorably to the removal of gluten include attention deficit disorder, celiac disease, autism, schizophrenia, and other autoimmune conditions such as fibromyalgia and multiple sclerosis. There are other foods that may cause reactions similar to those by gluten and casein, such as soy, corn, and rice. These may also need to be eliminated from the diet or rotated, or eaten with enzymes to aid in their digestion. In many of these disorders, "leaky gut" causes a wide range of physical as well as behavioral problems. The removal of these offending foods can bring about dramatic changes!

Following a gluten-free, casein-free diet is not always easy, but it is *not* impossible! Acceptable food was once difficult to find, expensive, and not very tasty. However, within the last few years, this has begun to change, as awareness of special dietary needs increases. Health food stores stock many safe foods that are gluten-free and casein-free. Many grocery stores now stock safe foods as well. Homemade breads often taste much better than store-bought, and safe flours, such as rice, sorghum and tapioca are now much easier to find. There are numerous excellent cookbooks devoted to GFCF recipes.

In this story, Jason tells of how his grandma makes foods for him that are safe to eat, including pizza, bread, and muffins. His mommy bakes safe cupcakes for him so he can bring his own special cupcake to school on days when there is a birthday celebration. Jason is happiest when he is just like all the other kids.

Many home bakers have discovered that it is *not* difficult to bake GFCF bread that is better than bread found in stores. Many home bakers have found success with baking muffins, cookies, crackers, cakes, pancakes, and even English muffins. These homemade products taste good, and are usually less expensive than the products found in stores. It is important to find a good gluten-free cookbook and read it cover to cover before trying your hand at baking.

Children want to be just like other kids, so it is important to find safe snacks that they can enjoy at home and at school. Fruits and vegetables are usually acceptable. Most kids like chips, and those who cannot have gluten can usually have corn and potato chips, rice crackers, or cereals made with safe grains. Many children with leaky gut have multiple food allergies or sensitivities, however, so keep that in mind when looking for safe alternatives.

Many new consumer laws are making it easier to determine whether or not gluten or casein are present in food. In the near future, it will become mandatory for labels to specifically list all possible allergens and potential sources of gluten or casein. ALWAYS READ LABELS! Some corn chips contain buttermilk. Some rice cereals contain wheat. Many crackers and cookies and cereals may be made from rice, but barley is added as a sweetener. **Just because a product is labeled "wheat-free" does not mean that it is gluten-free. And just because a product is labeled "dairy-free" or "milk-free", does not mean it is casein-free!** Always call the manufacturer to check the source of ingredients, such as "natural flavors" or "modified food starch".

One of the most frustrating parts of attempting to go gluten-free and casein-free is that gluten and casein are found in so many non-food products. They can be found in play-dough, glue, soaps, shampoos, stickers, toothpaste, vitamins, other medications, spices, flavorings, and on and on. Most of these products are available in GFCF varieties. They can be readily found in health food stores or ordered through the internet. It is vitally important that you become a label reader. If you are not sure about the ingredients on a label, just call the manufacturer; customer service representatives can usually tell you whether or not their products are GFCF.

Cross-contamination is another problem that faces would-be GFCF families. Many manufacturers use flour to dust their conveyor belts, thus contaminating an otherwise "safe" food. Some companies will not verify their products to be GFCF if they are stored in the same room as flours and other gluten products. Buying at bulk food stores can be dangerous, too, for the same reasons. Cross-contamination can also be a problem at home. Make sure that toaster ovens, utensils, and other baking items are kept separated from foods containing gluten or casein.

Families often feel unable to go out to eat at restaurants. However, there are many restaurants that are perfectly safe to visit. Ask questions! Make sure the waitperson knows your food issues. Ask to speak to the chef. When ordering a hamburger, for example, make sure that it is 100% beef without any fillers, and that the meat patty is grilled away from where the buns have been toasted. Order salads without croutons or cheese. Ask how the food is prepared. Many fast food restaurants are aware of the problems caused by food sensitivities, and have dedicated fryers to keep their French fries separated from their onion rings. Now Jason can even enjoy fast food; he just orders his hamburger without a bun and has fries on the side! Many restaurants now offer gluten-free menus.

There are many support groups, websites, and cookbooks that can be very helpful when starting a GFCF diet (some are listed at the end of this guide). Making a healthy choice for your child does not have to taste bad. GFCF food can still be enjoyed! Great-tasting substitutes and new foods can replace those that once made your child feel sick or caused behavioral changes. Your child need not feel excluded when peers eat foods containing gluten or casein. The effort of following the GFCF diet will soon be forgotten when the rewards of a healthier lifestyle become apparent. Just as Jason realized it wasn't so hard being on the GFCF diet and that he preferred not to eat the foods that made him feel sick, so may your child begin to grow and be nourished by the healthy GFCF food he or she eats!

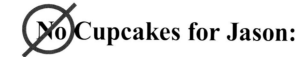 # No Cupcakes for Jason:

A School Guide to the GFCF Diet

Until now, Jason has lived in the safe environment of his home, where his food, meals and snacks are closely monitored by his parents. Now that he is five years old, and has started kindergarten, his whole world has opened up. Now food is everywhere - even in the classroom, and other places in his school.

Many classroom teachers use food as a reward. A child has a good day, or attains a certain number of stars, and he can choose a prize. Many times the prize is a piece of candy or stickers. Sometimes, teachers use food for teaching math games (counting M & M's, etc.). Art teachers use cereal and other food items for projects. We all remember taking the attendance sheet to the office secretary and being rewarded with a cookie. The ladies in the cafeteria often will give out left-over "goodies" at the end of the day. A substitute teacher might bring a bag of lollipops or other treats for the children who have been particularly cooperative that day. Food is everywhere. Now Jason is in this big world of his and he must be responsible for making so many decisions. He must be taught to ask, "Is this gluten-free?" This is a large burden to put on the small shoulders of a five year-old. But, to feel well and to be safe, he must do it.

In this age of food allergies, school personnel must realize that food must be more carefully distributed. Certainly, this does not imply that all food should be eliminated from the school day, or that children with no known food disorders should go without treats during the school day. It does mean, however, that all school personnel must be aware that there are children who cannot tolerate some foods, and that no food should be given to children without first checking with the classroom teacher. Of course, parents have the ultimate responsibility of instructing the classroom teacher as to what foods their child can and cannot tolerate. Perhaps the safest and easiest way of doing this would be to include it in the child's IEP (Individualized Education Plan). If a child does not require such a plan, then the parents should provide written notice of the child's dietary needs to the teacher, the paraprofessional, the "specials" teachers, office personnel, and any other school staff who might expose the child to gluten or casein.

Unfortunately, a list of exposed hazards should not stop at food. There are many other products found in an average classroom that may contain gluten. Gluten can be found in play-dough, on the adhesive of stickers and stamps, in crayons, glue, paste, markers, paint, and tape. A child sensitive to gluten does not have to ingest it to have adverse reactions. A sticker with adhesive that has gluten in it just has to touch the child's skin to provoke reactions. A child merely has to touch play-dough to have a bad reaction. The important thing to remember is that almost all of the above products can be found in gluten-free varieties. Gluten-free play-dough can be easily made. Stickers can be given to a child on a piece of paper - not put on the skin – and be considered safe.

It becomes so very important to keep the lines of communication open between the parent and the school regarding food sensitivities. As discussed in the Parents' Guide, when there are plans to bring food to school, the parents of the food-sensitive child should be informed in advance so that the child can bring in his own "safe" cupcake. If macaroni would be used in an art project, ask the parent of the food-sensitive child to provide gluten-free pasta. Parents should also be asked to supply the school with a list of safe products that are used on a daily basis in school: safe markers, safe glue, safe paste, and safe paint. Many parents with a child who is sensitive to gluten or casein have an entire shopping guide that provides this kind of information. If it is not possible to supply the "safe" products for the entire class, then at least ask the parent of a gluten-sensitive child to bring in his own supplies and keep them separated from the rest of the students' supplies.

If you have reason to believe the gluten-sensitive child has suffered a gluten infraction, be sure to call the parent as soon as possible. There are measures that a parent can take at home to try to minimize potential problems. Be sure that the parent knows what has happened, to help avert volatile behaviors, sleepless nights, rashes, diarrhea, and other problems.

Please remember that a child with food allergies or sensitivities must be able to feel safe in school. This child will be spending many, many years in a school setting. The school becomes the second most important place in his life, after his own home. He must know - even at five years old - that he can go to school and still feel well and healthy. He must feel protected and safe. This becomes an awesome responsibility for the school staff, but not an impossible one. Ask questions, read available materials about the GFCF diet, and most of all, talk to the parents of all your students.

Resources

DeHart, Judy. "GFCF Diet: Dietary Intervention for Autistic Spectrum Disorders" [ONLINE] Available www.gfcfdiet.com 2005.

Fenster, Carol. Special Diet Solutions: *Healthy Cooking Without Wheat, Gluten, Dairy, Eggs, Yeast or Refined Sugar, 3rd edition.* Savory Palate: 2001.

Hagman, Bette. The Gluten-Free Gourmet Bakes Bread. New York: Henry Holt & Company, 1999.

Hicks, Dr. John and Betsy. "Pathways Medical Advocates" Offering medical and diet counseling. (262) 740-3000, www.pathwaysmed.com 2005

Korn, Danna. Kids with Celiac Disease: *A Family Guide to Raising Happy, Healthy Gluten-Free Children* Woodbine House, 2001.

Lewis, Lisa and Seroussi, Karyn. "ANDI: Autism NDI- Autism Network for Dietary Intervention" [ONLINE] Available www.autismndi.com 2005.

Lewis, Lisa Phd. Special Diets for Special Kids Arlington: Future Horizons, 1998.

McCandless, Jaqueline. Children with Starving Brains: *A Medical Treatment Guide for Autism Spectrum Disorder,* Second Edition Bramble Books, 2003.

Prohaska, Betsy. Cooking Healthy Gluten and Casein-Free Food for Children. Book and VHS video, 2001. Available by ordering from www.pathwaysmed.com

Rapp, Doris MD Is This Your Child? Perennial Currents; 1st Quill edition, 1992.

Seroussi, Karyn. Unraveling the Mystery of Autism and Pervasive Developmental Disorder: *A Mother's Story of Research and Recovery.* New York : Simon & Schuster, 2002.

Shaw, William, MD. Biological Treatments for Autism and PDD. Sunflower Publishing, 2001.

About the Authors

Writing ~~No~~ *Cupcakes for Jason* has been a real family project. Co-author Judith Crane has spent the better part of the last forty years in the field of education. Early on she was an elementary school teacher, and later she worked as a school social worker. She has also worked as a substitute teacher, a tutor and a special ed para-educator before retiring three years ago. She is an avid reader and spends part of every week babysitting and baking for her three grandsons. She lives in Royal Oak, Michigan.

Judith's daughter, Stephanie Harlan, is co-author. Stephanie is a social worker and director of a non-profit resource center, and she volunteers much of her time to helping parents of special needs children. She is the mother of five-year-old Justin and wife of Kevin, who is the illustrator of this book. Kevin also works in the field of education and is an avid chess player. The Harlans make their home in Berkley, Michigan.